Save It For Me
Good Vibrations Book 3
Copyright © 2016 by Emma D. Fallon
ISBN: 9781682307199

EverAfter Romance

Without limiting the rights under copyright reserved above, no part of this publication may be reproduced, stored in or introduced into a retrieval system, or transmitted, in any form, or by any means (electronic, mechanical, photocopying, recording, or otherwise) without the prior written permission of the above author of this book. This is a work of fiction. Names, characters, places, brands, media, and incidents are either the product of the author's imagination or are used fictitiously. The author acknowledges the trademarked status and trademark owners of various products referenced in this work of fiction, which have been used without permission. The publication/ use of these trademarks is not authorized, associated with, or sponsored by the trademark owners.

T0169413

This part of Caroline and Tom's story is dedicated
to the wives, girlfriends, lovers, mothers, sisters, daughters and friends
of the soldiers who fought in Southeast Asia from 1955-1975.
We know that for some, the war never ended.
For those whose wait didn't end, for those whose wait ended in tragedy and loss,
and for those whose wait was actually just the beginning of a new war . . .
may you find peace and healing.

"Yet, finally, war is always the same. It is young men dying in the fullness of their promise. It is trying to kill a man that you do not even know well enough to hate . . . therefore, to know war is to know that there is still madness in this world."

President Lyndon B. Johnson
State of the Union Address
January 12, 1966

Tom and Caroline met on a summer day in 1965 in Ocean City, New Jersey. He was a soldier about to be sent to Vietnam. She was a divorceé whose future was uncertain. For just one night, they gave each other everything . . . and then said goodbye.

But not all goodbyes are forever.

Six months and many sizzling-hot letters later, Caroline and Tom are together again, this time in paradise. Tom's R&R feels like heaven on earth, a place where war doesn't exist. Neither of them want these seven days—and nights—to ever end.

For one week in Hawaii, the past is irrelevant and the future is forgotten as two lovers share their hearts, their souls and their bodies under Pacific skies.

Chapter One

I felt his fingers on me even before I opened my eyes. For one dizzying, disoriented moment, I didn't know where I was, and panic surged through my heart before I remembered it all with wonderful clarity.

I wasn't in New Jersey, in my own lonely bed. I was in Hawaii, and Tom, the most amazing, wonderful man in the world, the man I loved, the man who somehow loved me, too, was here with me, his broad chest pressed against my back, his chin touching the top of my head, and his very talented fingers circling my stiff nipple.

"Hmmm." I snuggled into his embrace. "This is not a bad way to wake up."

"It's about time." Tom's voice was gruff with sleep, and it sent a thrill up my spine. The one and only time we'd spent the night together, he'd already been up and dressed by the time I'd woken up. I hadn't gotten to discover what it was like to slowly come aware in his arms, so now I was relishing every nuance.

"Sorry. I thought I'd be up early because of the time difference, but I guess I was still exhausted from the trip." It was hard to believe that it had only been the day before that I'd arrived on the island, that Tom and I had only been together here for about twelve hours. There was a delicious soreness between my legs that reminded me of how well we'd used that time. "Didn't you sleep well? I'd have thought you'd be wiped out, too."

"I was. And I did." He swept my hair off my neck and nibbled on the side of my throat. "But for me, it's . . ." He lifted his head to see the small white clock on the bedside table. "Hmm. Two in the morning. So I guess I should be sleeping, after all." He dropped back to the pillow. "Good night."

"Hey." I shifted onto my stomach, bracing myself on my elbows and looking down into Tom's face. His eyes were closed in feigned sleep, but the corners of his lips twitched. I touched the edge of his chin, rubbing the bristles of his whiskers with the tip of my finger. "You're supposed to be catering to my every sexual need, aren't you? Isn't that what you promised me last night?"

A broad grin spread over his face, and his eyes slid open. "I did make you a promise, didn't I? So do you feel like I'm not living up to that?"

"Well . . ." I laid my head down on his chest, pressing my ear against his reassuring heartbeat. "Here I am. Naked. Laying on top of you. And you're pretending to be asleep. That doesn't feel very productive."

"You're absolutely right." He wrapped his arms around me and rolled so fast that I was on my back before I could react. "This is no way to celebrate the very first morning we get to wake up together, with neither of us leaving."

I could feel his erection between us, just above the juncture of my legs. "This is definitely more like it."

Tom chuckled a little, but I could tell his attention was elsewhere . . . specifically, on my boobs. And that was fine with me, especially when his mouth followed suit. He pressed a kiss just above one nipple before he traced a circle around it with the tip of his tongue. I shivered and tried to shift so that he'd get closer to where I wanted him.

"Patience, baby." The vibration of his voice, low and intimate, against my skin sent a thrill of pure want down to my core. Patience never had been my strong suit.

But Tom ignored my low groan of frustration and continued to rain tiny kisses all over one breast, moving down the slope and repeating the action on the other side. I arched my neck and closed my eyes, focusing on the sensation of his mouth almost reverently touching me.

Finally, after moving his lips in ever-smaller circles, he hovered over the aching pink tip that craved him. His eyes flickered up to meet mine and hold my gaze as he lowered his mouth over the nipple and sucked hard.

I moaned again, this time in pleasure, and threaded my fingers together at the back of his neck, holding him in place. His tongue pressed the stiff bud into the roof of his mouth, and his teeth gently scraped there, only heightening the feel. When Tom moved his lips to the other nipple, his hand went to work on the one he'd just abandoned, rolling it between one finger and thumb.

"You have the most beautiful tits. I thought maybe I'd just imagined how great they are, but actually, my memory didn't do them justice." He lay his head on my stomach, palming one boob and watching as the nipple stiffened when he traced a circle around it.

"You didn't have a long time to get to know them." I cupped his cheek with one hand, smiling a little as I glanced down at him. "So you're forgiven if you were a little hazy on some details."

"Hmmm." He turned his head to lick against the heated skin just above my navel. "Maybe we should take some pictures this time." He grinned, raising an eyebrow as he wriggled lower on my body. "Hey, you're the photographer now. Here's a job for you."

I laughed. "Buddy, if you think I'm going to take naked pictures of myself—or let you do it—and then have them developed at the store, you've got another think coming. I'd die of embarrassment."

"And you think I'd be okay with letting other guys see your naked pictures? No way, babe. I have a better idea. Tell you . . ." He slid both hands between my thighs and parted my legs. "Later."

Without waiting for me to respond, he lowered his mouth to cover the part of my body he'd taught me to call my pussy. I'd never known names for those body parts, slang or otherwise, until my night with Tom, but now the words now flowed off my tongue.

And speaking of tongues . . . what Tom was doing with his, on my pussy, was about to make me lose my ever-loving mind.

He licked me once, firmly, holding my thighs open with his hands, nudging further apart to give him better access. His fingers massaged the taut muscle there, and his lips fastened on the small button of nerves that throbbed for his touch.

"Tasting you is the most amazing thing I've ever done in my life. Do you know that?" His tongue darted down to my opening, tracing the edge before thrusting into me. "And feeling you come against my mouth is incredible."

I writhed, holding his head against me. "Oh, you think you can do that? Make me come right now, with just your tongue?"

Tom paused, raising his head to look at me, one eyebrow cocked. "Don't you think I can?"

I loved that we could play like this, that our lovemaking was more than just a coupling of our bodies; it was fun, light and yet so meaningful. I massaged the back of his neck.

"Well . . ." I pretended to doubt. "I'm not saying you can't. But we could make it interesting."

One side of his mouth quirked up. "Just what did you have in mind, Miss Rogers?"

"Let me think." I closed my eyes. "You make me come with just your mouth, no fingers, and I'll . . ." I tried to think of something that would work as a reward. "I'll act out your most secret fantasy. The thing you've never told anyone."

Tom's eyes glittered with interest. "Really? My most secret fantasy? That could be pretty far outside your comfort zone, babe."

I traced his jaw with the tip of my finger, as far as I could reach. "I'm willing to take that risk."

"Challenge accepted." He settled himself back down between my legs and reaching up, threaded his fingers through mine, joining both our hands. "You hold on, just to keep me honest."

"Don't worry. I'll make sure there's no cheating." I gripped his hands. "I'm not going to make this easy for you. You probably don't know this about me, but I'm a pretty fierce competitor."

"Uh huh." He covered my center again. "Oh, and by the way, the deal is that I can make you come with just my mouth, right? So I can use my tongue . . ." He licked my clit, hard. "My lips . . ." He suckled at me. "And my teeth . . ." He bit lightly, nearly sending me into oblivion.

I focused on containing my pleasure, on tamping it down. I tried to think about anything except Tom's mouth as he tasted, tempted and teased my pussy. My jaw clenched, and I bit down on my lip.

"And you know what's really sexy?" His voice was husky, vibrating into my very being. "Slipping my tongue inside you, and while I'm doing it, looking up at you, watching your face. Seeing your tits, so fucking big and all flushed from where I was just sucking them, and your beautiful eyes, soft and hazy because—"

"Would you be quiet?" I ground out the words. "You're not playing fair."

He affected a look of innocence, which had to be pretty tough to do with his head between my legs. "You said I could use my mouth. Talking is using my mouth."

"Uggghhhh." I groaned. "You're killing me."

"Doesn't have to be that hard, babe. Relax. Give in. Both of us are winners." To hammer home his point, he opened his mouth over my folds and pressed his tongue against my clit before he spoke again. "When you do, you're going to come so hard, and then, while you're still so high up you feel like you're never coming down, when you're still pulsing, I'm going to slide inside you, fuck you so hard that you'll come again . . . and again."

"God!" I couldn't hold it back any longer. I couldn't stop. Unbearable ecstasy started at the spot where Tom's mouth met my center and shot up my spine, traveling in waves through my body. My hips lifted of their own accord, but Tom held me down and kept up his relentless assault. I squeezed his hands, still firmly linked with mine, until he wrenched them away, hoisted his body over me and was about to plunge into me when he stopped.

"Shit. Shit, shit, shit. I need a condom." Dropping to his side, he reached for the box on the nightstand and fumbled with the small packet. I was still too caught up in the throbbing pleasure to help him, but he managed to roll it over his jutting erection and position himself back over me again. Without any more prelude, he thrust himself home.

I cried out, wrapping my legs around his body and digging my heels into his ass. Tom pumped into me, his strokes hitting me in the perfect spot, so that I soared again, arching beneath him.

"Caroline . . . baby . . . God, I love you. Being inside you is like nothing I've ever had before. I just want to be in you . . . be part of you . . ." He dipped his head to kiss me hard. "Love you so . . . much."

He tensed then, his cock deep in me, his face contorting as he came. I watched him, studying the way his eyes shut and his mouth fell open a little as his breath came in short pants. And when he fell onto the bed—next to me, not on me—I gathered him close, kissing his forehead, his cheek and the spot where his hairline began.

"That was about the best way I've ever woken up." I nuzzled his neck, humming a little in contentment. "Even if I did lose the bet."

Tom's lips curved into a sleepy smile. "I think that was kind of a win-win deal. You did give it a good fight, though." He opened his eyes, shifting up to lie on his back. "And you have no idea, babe . . . I think of how you were when we met last summer. You've done just what I hoped and taken charge of your own sexuality. That's fucking hot, in case you didn't notice."

My face grew warm, and I was sure I'd flushed in appreciation of his compliment. "You're quite the teacher. And this was with you halfway around the world from me. Imagine what'll happen when we're together all the time. I might be dangerous."

Something I didn't quite recognize flickered in his eyes, vanishing before I could wonder about it. "That's very true. If I don't watch out, I could create a sex addict." His lip curled up. "Of course, there are worse things."

"True." I snuggled onto his chest, taking a moment to revel in the simple nearness of him, memorizing every nuance of the feel of his solid warmth beneath me. "So are you going to tell me about the fantasy I need to play out for you?"

Tom shook his head. "Not yet. I need to recover a little, and if we don't get out of this bed, you won't be able to walk. When you go home and people ask you how you liked Hawaii, you'll have to make something up to tell them."

"I'm not here for the scenery or the tourist spots. I'm just here to see you." I curled my fingers around his still-partially erect cock. "But I have to say, this scenery looks mighty fine."

He groaned. "You're going to kill me, woman."

I slithered down his body. "But what a way to go."

Chapter Two

"This was delicious, but I'm so full now." I pushed my plate back a little bit and sighed, gazing out the window of the small diner. "Look at those palm trees. You know, when I got here yesterday, all I could think about was you. Seeing you, touching you, talking to you . . . I almost forgot I was in Hawaii. It's crazy to think we're in the middle of the Pacific Ocean. It's so beautiful, everywhere you look."

Tom reached across the table and wove his fingers through mine. "Are you saying now that you remembered where you are, you're done with me? Tired of me already?"

I leaned forward, staring deep into his blue eyes, hoping I could convey the message I needed him to hear. "Never. I'm not tired of you, and I will never, ever be done with you. Not if I live to be a hundred and ten."

"Even though I'll be a hundred and thirteen, and possibly not capable of getting it up anymore?" He smirked, tightening his grip on my hand.

"Well . . . hmmm. Let me re-think this. If you're not going to be able to satisfy me in the way I've become accustomed—"

"'Accustomed?' One night last summer, and then last night, and suddenly you're accustomed to it?" One eyebrow quirked up.

"Yes." I nodded. "I'm the type of person who gets spoiled very easily."

Tom grinned and rubbed the back of my hand with his thumb. "I'm the type of guy who loves spoiling you. So that works out."

We sat there for a few minutes, smiling at each other like a pair of crazy people, just appreciating the simple joy of eating a meal together.

There had been so many firsts today. The first time we'd awoken together in bed. The first time we'd gotten ourselves ready to go out, sharing a bathroom, showering . . . together, of course. Tom had teased me about shower sex, but when I'd reached for him under the spray, he'd only laughed and held onto my upper arms, as though keeping me at a distance.

"Let's save something for tomorrow, shall we? We have a week. We should probably pace ourselves."

And when he'd pulled on a pair of khaki shorts and a polo shirt, I'd stared in unashamed admiration.

"What?" Tom had frowned at me, puzzled.

"I've never seen you in anything but your uniform." I'd reached up to touch his collar. "You look . . . so different. You don't look like the soldier I met on the beach in Ocean City. You look more like a guy from California."

He'd stroked my cheek with two gentle fingers. "I *am* a guy from California."

"Yes, but I don't know that guy. I only know the soldier." It had frightened me, suddenly. There was so much of Tom that was foreign to me. Unknown, even. I remembered with an inward shudder the autumn before when I hadn't heard from him for weeks. I'd been terrified that he'd been killed, but that I'd never know, since I was neither wife nor blood family.

"Hey." Tom had drawn me closer, nudging my chin until I looked up at him. "The soldier and the California guy—they're both the same person. They're both me. And you know me. You know me better than anyone else in the world, if you want the truth."

Now, watching him across the table, I thought of what he'd said back at the hotel. "Do you really think I know you so well? Better than anyone else in the world?"

As if he'd been reading my mind, Tom didn't ask me what I meant or how I'd happened to ask that question. "Yeah. I tell you things I've never shared with anyone else." He traced my knuckles with the finger of his other hand. "You're the most important person in the world to me, Caroline. I know that may sound crazy–"

"No." I shook my head. "The crazy thing is that it doesn't feel odd or wrong. It feels exactly right, and it's the same way I think of you. What you know about me—it's stuff I've never told anyone. I share parts of myself with you that I'd never even known existed."

"I know. I told Aunt Cissy that after I write to you, I feel like I know myself better than I did before. She said that's the sign of a real soulmate." He shook his head. "I probably shouldn't say anything like that."

But I was too busy being surprised to pick up on his last words. "You talk to your aunt about me?"

Tom shrugged. "Well, I write to her about you, yeah. Why wouldn't I? I've always told her everything—almost everything. Maybe not down and dirty details. Since you're important to me, and a big part of my life now, I couldn't really not say anything."

I was all at once charmed, smitten and utterly on fire. He'd talked about me to his family and to his friends. Tom had been so careful not to say or do anything that might make me feel too tied to him, but all the while, he was telling important people about us.

"What exactly did you say to Aunt Cissy about me?" I didn't care; I trusted Tom, but I wanted to know, anyway.

One of his eyebrows rose. "Hmmm. I told her that you're the most intelligent woman I've ever met. The most beautiful, too, of course. And I told her you have the perfect mouth for going down on my cock."

"Tom!" I was certain my face was red. "You didn't. I mean . . . you didn't tell her that we—what we did."

He released my hand and sat back, laughing. "Not in specifics, honey, but she's not stupid or naïve. When I told her I'd spent the night at your beach house with you, and then that we were going to be together this week in Hawaii, I'm pretty sure she knew we weren't just playing tiddlywinks."

I tilted my head. "You told her about this week?" It hadn't occurred to me that Tom had family and other friends who might have wanted to see him during his leave. My own selfishness appalled me. "Tom, I feel horrible. Didn't she want to come see you this week? She must hate me, for taking up this time."

"Caroline, stop." He fastened me with stern eyes. "Aunt Cissy understood, completely. She said she's happier knowing we're together this week than she would've been being here herself. I'll call her before I go back, and we'll be able to talk a little." He winked at me. "Maybe I'll put you on, too, so the two most important women in my life can meet across the lines, at least."

I was a little dizzy, but in the best way possible. "I wish I could meet her in person. From everything you've said, she's a wonderful person."

"Someday you will. I believe that." He lifted his arms over his head and stretched, yawning. "I think the time difference is catching up with me. That, or I ate too much breakfast. You ready to go? Maybe if we walk around a little bit, I'll feel more awake."

He tossed a few bills on the table and offered me his hand. We made our way out of the diner and onto the sidewalk, both of us blinking in the bright sunshine. We'd found this place by accident, after driving aimlessly around Honolulu for half an hour. It was situated about a block from the beach, where I could see endless blue water sparkling on the other side of a stretch of white sand.

"So . . . what'll it be? I heard we can walk around Diamond Head—I think it's about a twenty-minute drive. Or we can drive up to the North Shore. There's also some kind of Polynesian Cultural Center, I guess. And I'd like to see Pearl Harbor while we're here."

I squinted around us. "Maybe we could start with a walk on the beach and figure it out from there?"

Tom twined his fingers through mine. "That sounds like an excellent idea. After all, it's only right we should get in some beach time, right? Considering we met along the shore."

"True."

We followed the brick walkway around a hotel, through a parking lot and onto a spread of vivid green grass. I pressed my palm against the solid trunk of a palm tree as we passed, marveling at the feel of its bumpy bark under my hand. The fronds rustled overhead in the steady breeze.

"I can't believe how warm it is. They were expecting snow at home the day after I left, you know. I was so worried the storm might hit early and keep me from leaving."

"Thank God it didn't." Tom's voice was fervent. "I would've been going nuts, being here while you were stuck on the East coast."

We paused on the edge of the grass, and Tom steadied me while I unbuckled my shoes, looping the straps between the fingers of my free hand. I waited as he untied his sneakers, peeled off his socks and stuffed them into the shoes, and then we both stepped onto the sand with our feet bare.

"Oh, it's hot!" I hopped onto one foot. "But the sand is so much smoother than at home."

"In California, it's more like small pebbles than sand. This is like powder."

"Exactly." I tugged his arm. "Come on, let's get to the water before my toes blister."

What struck me most was how intense all the colors were here. The trees and the grass were such a bright green, and the water and sky so blindingly blue that it nearly made me cry. I sighed when we reached the wet sand, relieved to be off the hotter ground, but when the water flowed over my feet, that sigh turned to a gasp.

"Oh, my gosh! It's so cold."

Tom laughed. "It's the Pacific, babe. And it's January. Even though the air's warm, the ocean's always going to be pretty frigid."

"I guess swimming is out of the question." Shading my eyes, I gazed out to the horizon. "Shouldn't there be people surfing here? I always thought that was one reason people came to Hawaii, to ride the waves."

"Mostly on the North Shore, where the waves are bigger." He slid his arms around my ribs, drawing me back against him. "Maybe when we go up there, I can give you some surf lessons. What do you think?"

"I think if you think I'm getting into that freezing water, you've got a screw loose." I tipped my head back, looking at him upside down. "Let's walk a little bit."

We wandered in companionable silence for several moments before Tom spoke again. "So, I've been meaning to ask you. What did your parents say about you coming over here to see me?" When I didn't answer right away, he added, "You did tell them, didn't you?"

"Of course I did." I hesitated. "Well, I told my mother. And my sister."

"Ah." Tom's jaw tightened. "And . . .?"

"My sister said she hoped I knew what I was doing. My mother said that if my father found out, it might kill him, so I shouldn't say anything." I tried to keep the derision out of my tone. "Not that he'd be likely to notice if I were gone anyway. He rarely sees me."

"I'm sorry, Caroline." Tom gripped my hand a little bit firmer. "I didn't stop and consider what people might say. I just . . . I think of you as independent. I never thought that you coming over might be a problem for your family. I hope it doesn't make trouble for you at home."

"I don't live in my hometown anymore, so no one's likely to even realize I'm away. My sister Dee won't say anything, and you can be damn sure my mom won't, either. The only other people who know are my boss Paulie and my new friend Rose. They were both really excited for me. Rose even drove me to the airport."

"That's wonderful. I'm glad you've made friends." He smiled, although I noticed a trace of regret lingering in his eyes. "You know, babe, when I say I'm proud of you for how far you've come, I don't just mean in bed. You've moved out of your parents' house, gotten a job and made a whole new life for yourself. Most people wouldn't be so brave. You've got guts." He pulled me into his side and kissed the top of my hair. "Just one of the many things I love about you."

Hearing him say those words made my heart swell in my chest. Tom had finally told me that he'd loved me the night before. I'd suspected it was true, although I'd feared he wouldn't utter it out loud until he was safely home from Vietnam. "I never would've done any of it if I hadn't met you last summer. I knew what I wanted, but I was afraid to take hold of it. Afraid to take the risk. But even just those few stolen hours with you gave me the courage I needed to be me again." I thought about it for a minute. "Or maybe more accurately, me at last. I spent so long trying to please my parents, and then my ex-husband, that I never did get around to finding out what made me happy. Until you, that is."

"Making you happy is something I could do forever. And I'd love to spend my life helping you find out what you really want."

"What if all I really want is you?" I turned toward him, linking my hands behind his back and pressing my hips into his body. "What would you think if it turned out that being with you, being yours for all time, was the only thing I needed? Would you be disappointed?"

"Never." He dipped his head to touch his lips to mine. "But I have a feeling you're going to dream bigger than that." Threading his fingers through my hair, he studied me, his face serious. "I don't . . . it's hard for me to make plans right now. It feels like I have this giant boulder in my path, and I can't see around it yet. I think something might be on the other side, but I don't know for sure. As long as I have to be in Vietnam, my life is on hold."

"I know." I kissed his neck, just above the collar of his shirt. "I'm not asking for any commitments. Not yet. But I want to be with you until that boulder rolls off your path. Just don't push me away because you're afraid that I'm missing out on something, being with you."

"It would be the unselfish thing to do, I guess." Tom ran his hand down my back, rubbing gently. "But it turns out I'm not at all selfless when it comes to you. I want it all, and I'm willing to gamble with your future, too."

"Gamble away. Just now, I'm feeling pretty darn lucky." I arched my neck and pushed his face closer to mine, opening my mouth under his warm and seeking lips. "When it comes to the two of us, everything is all I'll take."

Chapter Three

"I don't think I've ever played tourist so much." I laughed as I glanced over my shoulder at Tom, who was coming through the hotel door behind me. "We packed a lot of sight-seeing into the last three days."

"We sure did." He shut the door and dropped onto the bed, his arms spread wide and his eyes closed. "I think you wore me out."

Stepping out of my shoes, I crawled up onto the bed next to him. "You mean with all the walking we've done? Or something else?"

He opened one eye and regarded me with speculative amusement. "I was referring to the sight-seeing, but I think a case can be made for both." Before I could register what he was up to, his hand snaked over to grasp my wrist and pull me so that I fell across him. "Not that I'm complaining, mind you. Not one fucking bit."

My face was very near his, and I took advantage of my position to kiss him. "Good, because I don't plan to stop wearing you out. In bed, at least. I'm pretty sure we've seen just about everything on this island."

"Maybe." He traced a line from my cheekbone to my chin. "I have a few other spots where I'd like to go, but we could take a day by the pool, too. Just relax a little bit."

"I'd like that." When I'd thought about our week together in Hawaii, I'd pictured only Tom and me, in bed together, talking, laughing and loving. I was surprised how much I'd enjoyed driving around the island with him and visiting all the standard tourist sites. We had gotten to know each other on an entirely different level, and incredibly, I was pretty sure I'd fallen even more deeply in love with him, something I hadn't thought was possible.

"How tired are you right now?" He cupped my face with one hand, guiding my mouth to his for an exploratory kiss. "Want a nap by the pool, or . . . do you want to stay in here, and not nap?"

"Hmmm . . . decisions, decisions." I pretended to consider. "You know, how often does a girl get to lounge by a pool in the tropical sunshine?"

"That's true. Whereas you can have truly spectacular sex whenever you want, huh?"

I giggled. "You make a good point." Running my hand down his side, I hummed a little in appreciation, my mouth curving into a wider smile as I cupped his very fine rear. "And you're willing to guarantee me this truly spectacular sex?"

"And then some." He flipped us over, grinding his hips into me so that I didn't have any doubt about how interested he was. His erection rubbed against my leg, and holding himself above me with one arm, he used the other hand to hike up my dress. "You know when we were on that tour where they grow the pineapples? All I could think about was getting back here and touching you. I could see your sweet little ass moving under this dress, and I just wanted to grab it."

He slid his fingers under my panties, moving them to suit his actions to his words, kneading my backside. "This right here? It was making me fucking crazy all afternoon. I was having wild daydreams about what I wanted to do."

"Daydreams? But you knew I'd be coming back here with you. It's not like I haven't been in your bed all week. And it's not as if you haven't been inside me every single night. And day. You don't have to dream when you have the real thing, ready, willing and able."

"Doesn't matter. Doesn't mean I don't still have fantasies about what I want us to do." He nuzzled my neck, growling softly. "You turn me on, baby. Like no one I've ever known."

Heat rose in my chest, a mix of arousal and pleasure. "I think you can tell I feel the same way."

"Only one way to find out." Tom's hand crept around to delve into my slick folds, his thumb finding the small bundle of nerves that craved his touch. "Oh, yeah. I'd say you're definitely on the same page I am."

"Page . . . paragraph . . . line . . ." I gasped as his fingers stroked me with steady surety. "Whatever. Just don't stop what you're doing."

"Not planning on it." Tom shifted a little, lying alongside me. He brought his lips close to my ear, murmuring to me even as his fingers continued to torment me. "You feel so good. Do you know how horny it makes me to touch you? When I feel how wet you are for me?"

"I know it's the most incredible thing I've ever felt, when your fingers are on me . . ." My voice trailed off as he took me even higher.

"That first night when we were together, and you didn't know how to tell me what you wanted, or even what it really was you wanted—I never could've guessed how great it would be between us. I thought I was going to be your teacher, but you've blown my mind."

"Is that a good thing?" The words came on a sharp intake as I arched my neck and closed my eyes.

"You better believe it is." Tom thrust two fingers into me, curling them so that he hit the spot that made me moan. "It's a fucking good thing, and there's no place I'd rather be than lying here with you, my hand on your pussy, my fingers inside you, feeling you squeeze around me—it's like we're part of each other." He touched the tip of his tongue to the damp skin of my neck. "And my dick is so hard, feels like it might explode."

"I can—I can help you with—ohhhhh." The moan turned into a cry as he increased both pace and pressure.

"You can help me by coming right now. Right now, against my fingers."

As though his words had been the only things holding me back, the climax ripped through me. I gripped Tom's arm, and my breath caught deep in my chest as nearly unbearable pleasure pulsed throughout me.

"That's it, baby. God, you're so beautiful. If I could take a picture of you right now . . ." A slow smile spread over his face. "That reminds me of my idea from the other day. About pictures."

Still naked, his cock stiff, Tom rolled off the bed and went over to open the closet door. Dragging out his duffle, he bent over and dug around for a minute before emerging with a box in his hand.

"What's that?" I lay on my stomach, my chin in my hands and my elbows sinking into the mattress.

"Something I bought right before I came over here. To Hawaii, I mean." He cast me a wry look, with a tiny bit of remorse laced through it. "Actually, I bought it from a soldier who needed the cash. I guess his sister sent it to him, but he wanted money for . . . well, I didn't ask what for, exactly. Didn't want to know."

Setting the box on the bed, Tom eased off the top, and I laughed when I saw what was inside. "A Polaroid?"

"Yeah. So we can take pictures of each other, even naked, and we don't have to have them developed. They're for our eyes only." He lifted the camera out of the box and touched a button so that it popped open. Glancing up at me, he quirked an eyebrow. "Don't move at all. Not one muscle."

I watched him as he fiddled with the camera, his forehead wrinkled in concentration and his mouth turned down in a slight frown. A new burst of love welled up in me; he looked so serious, so focused.

"Just like that." His whisper floated to me a second before the flash erupted, blinding me temporarily. Tom pulled out the picture and counted to sixty, slowly, before he peeled off the development paper.

"That's it." He held the photo up, his eyes resting on my image there. "That's what I want to take with me when I . . . when I go back." For the first time since we'd been together this week, I saw a glimpse of desperate pain on his face. I had a sudden flashback to our night together on the Jersey shore, when we'd been certain we'd never see each other again. Tom had refused to let me give him my address or to give me his; he didn't want to tie me down to a future he wasn't sure he could promise. I'd circumvented him by tucking a note with my address into his bag, but that hadn't happened until the next morning. I still remembered the exquisite agony of realizing I'd met the man who could be everything to me, only to learn that he was leaving to fight half a world away from me.

I reached up to take his hand and draw him back to me. "The picture's for later. Now, I'm here with you. You don't need a photo when you have the real McCoy."

He let me pull him down onto the bed with me and kiss him gently. With two fingertips, he brushed my cheek, my forehead and down the bridge of my nose, his eyes drinking me in as though he was trying to imprint me on his mind.

"You're right. I don't want to waste a single second of my time with you. Not when you're right here, in my arms."

His lips seared against mine as he poured every bit of emotion into the kiss. Gone was the light, teasing mood of a few minutes before; in its place was something deeper, something more real. His body covered me, taking me in, protecting me and at the same time drawing strength from me. I lay still beneath him, feeling him breathe as we both held tight to a moment that could never last long enough.

~~***~~

"Eating dinner in bed was the best idea ever." With my finger and thumb, I pulled a noodle out of the cardboard box, holding it over my head and letting it wriggle into my mouth. "What's this called again? The noodles?"

"Lo mein, my little East coast innocent." Tom smirked at me. "C'mon, try the chopsticks again. I promise, I won't laugh this time."

Rolling my eyes, I crossed my arms over my chest, covered only by a thin sheet. "We don't have Chinese restaurants in South Jersey. How in the world would I know how to use them? I didn't grow up near San Francisco, like you did."

This time, Tom laughed out loud. "No, babe, I lived in southern California. It's a long way from San Francisco."

"That's embarrassing." I picked up the smooth sticks and examined them. "I'm woefully ignorant about my own country's geography when it comes to the west. I can tell you all about New York and Pennsylvania and even New England, but then the rest is like . . ." I waved one hand vaguely. "Just out there. Los Angeles, the Grand Canyon, Las Vegas . . . it's somewhere, but I couldn't tell you where."

"That's not your fault. The lack is in the education system. But someday I'm going to take you all over California, and then into the desert in Arizona, and to the pueblos in New Mexico. Down the Strip in Vegas, and to Lake Tahoe to ski." Grinning, he tapped the end of my nose with one finger. "And of course, we'll go to Chinatown and have dim sum. So you better keep practicing with those chopsticks."

I fell back against the pillows. "Later. For now, I couldn't eat another bite."

"Not even a fortune cookie?" Tom held two in his hand.

"Not even. They're all yours."

"Hmmm." He cracked one open, revealing a small strip of white paper. "This one must be your fortune. It says, 'You are about to experience extreme pleasure.'"

"It does not." I made to grab for the paper, but Tom crumpled it in his hand.

"Bad luck to show someone else your fortune." He made a face of mock-regret.

I cocked an eyebrow. "I thought you said it was mine?"

"Could be it was meant for both of us." He leaned over me, his lips covering mine as they coaxed me to open. "As a matter of fact . . . I have an idea. Care to try something new?"

"Ooooh, that sounds intriguing." I teased the sides of his chest, where the muscles were tensed as he held himself over me. "After this week, I was pretty sure we'd done it all."

—

30

"Not even close, baby. Not even close. There're books we can work through, with different positions and uh . . . methods. But what I'm thinking about is pretty basic." As he spoke, Tom tugged down the sheet between us, baring my breasts to him. "God, I love your tits, baby. I just want to suck your nipples until you can't breathe for feeling good."

"That's something I think we did the other day. More than once, if memory serves."

"Memory does serve. And this isn't actually what I was talking about." Lifting his head, he laid his cheek between my boobs, his eyes meeting mine. "This is a mutual pleasure deal."

"Oh, and sucking my boobs doesn't do it for you?"

"Of course it does." His voice was fervent. "But this is a little more, um, immediate."

I wrapped my legs around his hips, kicking off the rest of the sheet. "Okay. Tell me what I need to do."

Tom rolled onto his back, one side of his mouth curled into a smile. "Straddle my face."

"Excuse me?" I thought I had an open mind, but this I hadn't expected.

"Facing my . . . feet."

I tilted my head. "All right. And then?"

He made a rolling motion with his hand. "One step at a time, babe."

I stifled a sigh and swung my leg over his head, resting my center on his chest, my knees bent alongside his shoulders. "Here I am. Now what?"

Reaching around me, he gripped his stiff cock, giving it one long stroke. "Now if you bend over, I think you might find something interesting to do with your mouth." One hand released his erection and skimmed up my thigh to my hip. "When you bend, scoot back a little bit. And I'll be able to do something interesting with my mouth, too."

I saw now where he was going with this, and it set me on fire. I leaned forward, adjusting myself until my lips hovered over the head of his cock.

"Wriggle back a little." His hands framed my backside, and I could feel his breath between my legs. I eased back until his lips met the sensitive flesh of my sex.

"Ohhhh." I moaned, arching my back. "This . . . this was a very good idea."

"Yeah." Tom's words were muffled, sending exquisite vibrations through me. I braced my hands on either side of him and lowered my mouth to envelop his dick.

If there was one thing I'd learned—or confirmed—in the past days, it was that I loved having my mouth on Tom's cock. In theory, I supposed it didn't sound like something I'd want to do. I couldn't imagine ever sharing this experience with my ex-husband. But the idea of giving Tom the pleasure of my mouth moving up and down over him set me on fire, and I loved the feel of his smooth skin beneath my lips, the slightly musky, addicting taste of him on my tongue and the sounds he made as I sucked him hard.

All that was heightened now by the fact that while I was giving him this gift, he was doing the same for me. He devoured my pussy, his mouth aggressive and relentless, his breath hot and his tongue agile and talented. There was something about the fact that we were doing this to—and for—each other that made the act even more sensual.

Drawing my mouth up, I hollowed out my cheeks and then circled the head of his dick with the tip of my tongue. Delicious pressure built low in my abdomen, a pulsing that told me I was about to plunge over the precipice. Groaning, I picked up my pace, balancing on one arm as I cupped his balls with my free hand, rolling them between my fingers.

"Babe, are you close? I'm going to come. God, I'm going to come so hard in your sweet fucking mouth."

"Yes." I ground out the single syllable, lifting my hips. "Yes—so close. Make me come now. Against your mouth, while I suck you dry."

With a growl that promised me sweet satisfaction, Tom thrust his tongue into me, scraping his teeth lightly over my clit.

Gratification exploded in every fiber of my body, and I shouted Tom's name, the sound garbled as he tensed in his climax. I swallowed the sudden flood of saltiness, the pulsing of his cock matching the throbbing between my legs.

Once he had stilled, I lifted my mouth from him and slid boneless onto the bed, my breath coming in rapid gasps. "What do you call that? Is there a name for it, or did you just make it up?"

Next to me, Tom's body shook with laughter. "No, baby, I didn't just make it up. It's called sixty-nine."

"Really? How come?" I laid a hand on his stomach, brushing my palm over the sculpted abs.

"Because if you're lying side-by-side doing that, we'd kind of look like that number. Get it?"

"I guess so." Pushing myself upright, I snuggled onto Tom's chest. "Have you done . . . that with a lot of other women?" I was only curious; I knew he'd had other lovers before me, and I wasn't threatened by the idea. Not when I knew that now, he only wanted me.

"Honestly?" He lifted his head, touching his lips to my hair, and then dropping back to the pillow. "Never. Not with anyone else. I'd heard of it, but I never felt comfortable trying it with any other woman. So you popped my sixty-nine cherry."

"Popped your what?" I frowned at him. There were so many phrases Tom used that I'd never heard, let alone understood.

"It means to lose your virginity. So I was a sixty-nine virgin, since I'd never done it before, and now neither of us are."

"Oh." I yawned. "I see."

"Hmmm." Tom's arm tightened around me. "And you know what I learned tonight, while getting my cherry popped? The combo of Chinese food and new experiences makes me really sleepy."

"Must be catching." I nuzzled his neck, sighing. "Maybe we just need to rest a little. Recharge."

"Maybe." His breath evened, but just before we both drifted off, I heard him murmur against my ear.

"Love you, Caroline."

Chapter Four

"We're starting to be regulars here." I sipped my coffee and lifted it in small salute to the diner. "Pretty soon, they'll know our names and recognize our orders."

He smiled somewhat ruefully. "Four days probably doesn't make us regulars, especially in a place like Honolulu, where they're used to tourists and soldiers."

I rolled my eyes. "Play along with me, please. I like the idea that someday, there might be a place where we go for breakfast every Saturday, and they get to know us so well, the waitress says, 'Hey, there, it's Caroline and Tom. You two want the usual?'"

I'd meant to make him smile, but instead, I saw the same fleeting expression in his eyes, something akin to uncertainty and pain. Reaching across the table, I snagged his hand, gripping it in my fingers.

"What's wrong?"

He smiled. "What in the world could be wrong? I'm sitting at breakfast on a beautiful island, with the most gorgeous, sexy and incredible woman I've ever known."

"Something's been on your mind all week. I can tell." A lump rose in my throat. "Is it me? Do you feel like I'm expecting too much, too soon? Am I pushing you into something you're not ready for yet?"

"Caroline." He brought his other hand up to cover our joined fingers. "Not at all. Not one little bit. As a matter of fact, it's . . . kind of the opposite."

"Okay." I caught the corner of my lip between my teeth. "I don't really get that. You're pushing me into something? I promise, I don't feel that way at all."

"No. What I mean is . . ." He drew in a deep breath, his gaze fastened on the table. "Before I got here, I'd thought about, when we were here, maybe . . . getting married."

I was so surprised that for a moment, I was sure I'd misunderstood him. Tom had been so cautious about letting me become too attached, so loathe to make plans beyond the present, that I never would've dreamed that marriage might cross his mind. Not now. Not yet.

"I know. It's crazy. But what happened last month, with the bombing and everything—it shook me up. I don't want to waste any time. I want us to be together, in every way we can."

Tears flooded my eyes. "I want that, too. It's all I want."

He went on speaking as though he hadn't heard me. "But then I realized how unfair that would be to you. Caroline, nothing has changed since we were together last summer. I still have over a year left on my tour in Vietnam. I can't be with you, I can't live with you, I can't support you. Not while I have this commitment. And what if I married you, and then you met someone else? You'd be stuck. You'd resent me."

"You're wrong, Tom." I ground out the words in frustration. "Don't you get it? It doesn't matter to me if we're married or not. I'm in love with you. I'm not going to meet anyone else, because for me, there are no other men. You are it for me, for the rest of my life. So marry me or don't, but it's not going to change how I feel, or the fact that I want you now and I will want you in a year, and I will want you in fifty years."

He closed his eyes and sucked in a ragged breath. "I kind of thought you'd say that. I feel the same, but still . . . like you said, getting married isn't going to change how committed I am to you. It's going to take up a bunch of precious time with paperwork, when all I want to do is be with you."

I could see his point. The last thing I wanted was to waste time dealing with bureaucratic red-tape when we could be alone together.

"And I want a real wedding with you. When I come home, I want to do it right. I want Aunt Cissy there, and your sister, and Paulie . . . and I hope your parents, if they'll come. But even if they don't, I still want to make it a big deal. White dress, rice and a church. I want our friends to decorate your Mustang so when we drive away, everyone can see that we just got married."

I grinned. "I don't think you'd look good in a white dress, Tom. Maybe ecru."

"Smartass." But he smirked, too. "Anyway, that's what I want." He hesitated a minute. "Unless you don't. You already had that, so maybe you'd rather have something quieter."

"I had the big wedding, but not the real marriage. This would be the real thing. I don't care if we get married on a mountaintop or in Westminster Abby. As long as you're the one who's saying I do to me, I'm in."

He studied me, a smile playing around his lips. "I love you, Caroline Rogers. And I'm going to love you for the rest of my days."

"Well, that's convenient, since I'm planning on loving you forever and day. And then maybe another week, just for good measure."

Tom stood up a little and leaned across to kiss me. "What do you say we head over to the Polynesian Cultural Center today? We'll soak up some of the culture, improve our minds and then . . ." He lowered his voice. "And then we'll go back to the hotel and pretend we're on our honeymoon."

"I like the way you think."

~~~***~~~

The Polynesian Cultural Center was interesting. Considering that I hadn't been sure of the location of San Francisco, it wasn't surprising that my knowledge of Hawaiian history was extremely limited. I listened intently as the guides taught us about different aspects of life in Polynesia, with the unfamiliar words filtering into my brain.

We'd just finished touring the Maori section when Tom tugged on my hand. The rest of the crowd sauntered to the next stop as we lingered behind.

"Did you miss something here?" I smiled up at him. "Didn't you get your fill of Maoris?"

"I think I got the gist of it. But before we move on to the Samoans, I've decided it's time to collect on the bet I won the other day."

I'd nearly forgotten about that. "Here? Now?"

He pulled me against him, wrapping his arms around my waist. "We agreed that the prize was you fulfilling my most secret fantasy, right?"

I cocked my head. "And your most secret fantasy is making out in a Maori village?"

"No." He laughed softly. "My fantasy is more ambitious than that. I want to fuck you in public. Well, in a public place."

My mouth dropped open. "Are you serious? Tom, what if we get caught?"

"We won't." He guided me around the corner of a building, toward an area shaded by palm trees. "I was checking it out while the guide was talking. Back here, no one can see us. Or hear us." He brushed my hair away from my face. "I promise I'd never put you in a position where you could be embarrassed. But isn't there a little bit of a turn-on to think about the possibility of discovery?"

I thought about it for a moment. "Maybe. I don't know. It makes me a little nervous."

"I could probably take your mind off that." Backing me against the building, Tom framed my face with his hands and slanted his head before he lowered his mouth to mine. His kiss was soft at first, just a simple meeting of our lips, and then he probed gently with his tongue, seeking entry. I opened to him, meeting each touch and tease.

As always, when Tom was this near to me, everything else in the world disappeared. I gripped his shoulders and lifted myself even closer to him.

"Kissing you is my all-time favorite activity." He skimmed his lips down my throat. "Although having my hands on your tits is a close second." So saying, he cupped my boobs over my dress, caressing my nipples with his thumbs. "When you get hard here . . ." He covered one side with his palm. "I go hard here." He caught my hand and brought to his cock.

I closed my fingers around him, through the thin cotton of his shorts. "Mmmmm . . . I like this."

"Me, too." His fingers pinched the hem of my short dress and inched it up. "You know what I like even more?" He slid under my panties. "When I find you wet and ready for me, right here. When you're practically dripping with wanting me."

Dropping my head back against the wall, I closed my eyes. "God, it feels so good when you touch me there."

". . . and over here, we have what would be a typical home from a Maori village. If you gather right on this grass, our dancers will perform a traditional dance of their culture."

The guide's voice was full of pep and cheer, and my eyes flew open in alarm. She sounded as though she was only a few feet away from us.

"Shhh." Tom laid a finger over my lips. "They can't see us. And in a minute, when the music starts up, they won't be able to hear us, either."

He bent his finger, slowly and softly stroking me with one hand while the other dropped from my mouth back to the neckline of my dress, delving beneath the material to find one turgid peak. He pinched the nipple, and when my mouth fell open again, he took advantage and kissed me, his lips hard and aggressive.

When he broke away, it was only to lean closer, murmuring into my ear. "I'm going to take you hard against this wall, and you better come fast, because I know I will. I want to be inside you, deep inside you."

The speakers on the front of the hut crackled and buzzed, and almost immediately, the canned music began. Tom fumbled to unzip his shorts, releasing his erection. My breath hitched, and my heart pounded.

"Lift up your dress a little." He stroked himself as I obeyed with shaking hands. Once the edge of my dress was hiked up to my hips, Tom pushed aside the crotch of my underwear and thrust inside me.

Sensations assaulted me. The loud music was only a few feet away from us, but all I could hear was my own pulse in my ears. Tom's fingers dug into my hip, holding me steady, and for the very first time ever, he was inside me with nothing between us. A small part of my very distracted brain wondered if he realized he hadn't put on a condom, but no way in hell was I going to bring that up now. Not when I could feel him in me, so close, so hard and so deep. Holding onto his arms, I let myself go to enjoy the ride.

He hadn't been kidding when he said we were both going to come fast. Whether it was the dangerous allure of possible discovery or simply that we were both incredibly aroused, I felt the irresistible rising of my own climax, and I bit down hard on my lip as my pussy clamped down his plunging cock.

Tom grunted low in his chest and froze, his jaw tensing as he let go, erupting inside me. I buried my face in his neck, trying to calm my breathing and keep from sliding onto the ground beneath us.

"Let me find my handkerchief." He withdrew from me, grimacing, and then dug into his pocket and pulled out the white cotton square. We were silent as he cleaned us both, zipped up and helped me straighten my dress. Just beyond us, the music played on.

"Caroline, thank you." He held my arms, gazing down on me with hooded eyes. "I know that wasn't exactly something you were comfortable trying, but God, it was incredible. I'll never forget it."

I stood on my toes to kiss him. "I'm not saying I want to make a habit of having sex in public, but it was definitely something new. I like stretching my boundaries, sometimes. With you anyway." I considered for a moment. "And I think doing it here, in Hawaii, where no one knows me, makes it a lot easier. If I were home, I'd be terrified my mom or one of my old high school teachers might walk around the corner and catch us. Now that would be humiliating."

"I'd never do that to you." He tipped up chin and rubbed his thumb over my lips. "Here, it's like a time and space set apart."

"True." I glanced over my shoulder as the recorded music faded away. "Think it's safe for us to sneak out yet? Or rejoin the tour?"

"Yeah, that other group is moving on. Want to catch up with them?"

I shrugged. "I wouldn't mind heading back to the hotel and maybe taking a swim, if you don't mind. I'm hot."

A slow smile spread over his face. "Yes, you are."

"Oh, you're just being naughty now." I rolled my eyes, even as I was sure a blush was creeping up my cheeks.

"I am. And you know that's how you love me." Tom took my hand, and we began walking back toward the parking lot.

"Tom." I spoke tentatively. "You know just now . . . that was the first time you didn't use a rubber."

"I know." He stroked my knuckles with one finger. "I didn't have one with me, and I thought, just this once, with you on the Pill, it would be okay. Plus, we were standing up, and that's not a very good position for getting pregnant." He hesitated. "Not that it's impossible, but you know my buddy Ben? I told you he and his wife wanted to have a baby. They're supposed to be here for R & R next month, and Ben said his wife was doing all kind of research with her doctor and at the library into the best way to conceive. What we did wasn't one of the recommended positions."

I thought about that. When I'd been married, James and I had talked about having children, but always as a someday kind of thing. Something that might happen in the future. James had told me that when it was meant to be, it would happen, but I'd thought to myself, Not when I'm on birth control, it probably won't. When I'd mentioned getting off the Pill, he'd said it wasn't a good time yet. And then shortly thereafter, he'd announced that he and his secretary were expecting a baby. I guess it had been a good time for them.

I was relieved that I'd never pushed the issue with my ex-husband, that no accidents had happened to bring us a baby. But the idea of carrying Tom's child within me brought with it a yearning so strong, I nearly burst into tears. I wished that we were already married, that we, too, had decided to try for a baby on this trip. That when I went back to New Jersey, it might be with the hope that I wasn't alone any longer. That I'd have a little bit of Tom with me, a small being who would be the best of both of us.

I knew it wasn't smart. We weren't married, and getting pregnant out of wedlock didn't happen for nice girls like me. Then again, getting divorced wasn't supposed to happen to us either.

"Hey." Tom drew me against his side as though he could hear my thoughts. "Someday that's going to be us. I'll get through this next year or so, and then we'll make plans. We'll have that big wedding, and before too long, we'll have those babies we talked about last summer."

I remembered all too well Tom's words that night, those wistful, anguishing might-have-beens that had both sustained me and killed me in the weeks after he'd left.

Beautiful blonde-haired babies, pretty and smart as their mom. I think we'd have a girl first, and then a boy, and we'd buy a house right on the beach so they could both learn to surf. And every night, you and I would take a long walk together on the beach, and we'd tell each other about our day. Then after the kids were in bed, I'd make love to you over and over, so you'd never forget how beautiful and sexy you are, and how much I love you. . .

"Sometimes it seems like that's a very long time away." I tried hard not to think of the fact that in two days, we'd be saying good-bye again, both of us leaving this piece of paradise to fly halfway around the world in opposite directions.

"I know." Tom tightened his grip on my hand. "But God, it's the only thing I can hold onto right now. It's the only thing making life possible. If I can't hold onto you and all those dreams, Caroline, I don't have anything."

His voice was filled with pain, and I swallowed hard over the lump in my throat. "We'll hold on. Both of us . . . we'll hold on as long as we have to, until we don't have to say good-bye ever again."

Chapter Five

I could remember when Hawaii was added to the United States. It hadn't even been ten years before, and I'd been getting ready to start my junior year in high school. My geography and history teachers had been thrilled, and they'd both taught units that year on the South Pacific and the importance of the Hawaiian Islands.

Still, in my head, all I'd ever pictured when I'd thought of Hawaii was Waikiki Beach: the ocean, the white sand and the palm trees. During my days here with Tom, though, I'd come to realize how much more this island was.

We'd driven into the mountains and stood in the breeze, ventured to the Windward Side to see Hanauma Bay, where the fish had swum right up to us for bread crumbs, spent an afternoon at Pearl Harbor, paying tribute to the brave men and women who had died in December of 1941. I'd come to realize that this small piece of real estate in the middle of the Pacific Ocean was more than just a beach and waves.

Today, on our very last day together, we'd decided to drive up to the North Shore. I'd jokingly suggested to Tom that we could just spend our last twenty-four hours together in bed, but he'd shook his head.

"I want to make more memories with you. Tonight we'll make love as long as we can both stay awake, but today, I want to soak in some more of the beauty of this place. I want to see you among the flowers, laughing, with the wind blowing your hair as you smile at me."

So here we were standing in a grotto near Waimea Falls, listening as a native Hawaiian woman sang a hauntingly beautiful song while younger girls performed a slow and sensuous hula. The water splashed into the pool at its base, purple orchids bobbed nearby, and I nearly cried from the breathtaking loveliness of it all. Tom's hand gripped mine tightly; I wondered if he were feeling the same anguishing perfection of this place.

The song came to an end, and the small crowd applauded. People began to move away, each group wandering in a different direction. Tom led me further into the trees, wrapping one arm around my shoulders as we stepped carefully on the narrow path.

"Do you have a nefarious agenda, sir, for getting me alone?" I shot him a saucy smile, winking.

He laughed. "I'd like to say yes, but this time, I only wanted to see a little more of the forest here. It's so beautiful."

"It is." I stopped beneath a tree and drew in a deep breath. "And it smells so good. I think this is what heaven will smell like, you know? Orchids and crystal clear water and sunshine."

"Maybe." Tom was distracted. I could tell by the way his eyes were distant and clouded. "If you were with me, it would definitely be heaven."

I leaned into him, sighing. "Can we just stay here? Hide where no one can find us?"

He chuckled, but the sound was strained. "If only. But we'd both get hungry after a while."

"You'd sneak out and get us burgers."

"I guess I could. And what would happen when the Army realized I was AWOL and came hunting for me?"

I closed my eyes and snuggled closer. "We'd climb up there in the trees and they'd never find us. We could be like the Tarzan and Jane of the South Pacific."

"They don't wear many clothes, do they?" He skimmed a hand down my spine. "I think I could handle that."

For the space of a few precious minutes, we stood there, still and alone, among the trees. Silence surrounded us; the rest of the group had moved on, and the only thing I could hear was the soft call of a few birds and the infinite flow of water into the quiet pool beneath the falls.

"I made a mistake." Tom's words ripped into the quiet.

Lifting my head, I stared up at him. "What do you mean?"

"I made a mistake, saying we shouldn't get married this week. We could've had another wedding, another celebration once I got home. But we should've gone ahead and said our vows while we were here. I wish I were leaving this island as your husband, not just a soldier you met accidentally last summer and slept with for a week on R & R."

I stiffened. "If that's what you think you are to me, you're insane. How can you say that?"

Tom slumped. "I know that's not fair or accurate. I'm just . . . I don't want to go back. I don't want to leave you. I never want to say good-bye to you again."

"I want that, too." I laid my ear onto his chest, listening to the steady and reassuring beat of his heart. "But even if we'd gotten married this week, you'd still be going back to Vietnam tomorrow. And I'd still be flying home alone." Tears filled my eyes. "So there's no use in wasting time thinking what might have been. We made the best of every possible minute this week. That's really all we could ask."

"But I want to marry you. Now." He cupped my face in his two hands. "I want to make vows to you here and now, promises I'll never break."

I covered his hands with mine, smiling into his eyes. "Then do it. What difference does it make if we're here, surrounded by trees and flowers and water and nature, in the presence of God, or if we're in a church with people and a minister? What I say will be more real, more me, here than it would be in front of an audience. I've already made you promises that I'm never going to break. Why not here? Why not now?"

Tom's mouth tilted at one corner into a half-smile. "Why not, indeed." He drew in a deep breath, and leaning his forehead against mine, he spoke words that would be forever etched into my heart and my soul.

"I, Thomas Andrew Lawson, take you, Caroline, to be my own forever and ever. I promise that I will take care of you, teach you and learn from you, cherish you, treasure you and love you all the days of my life. As long as I live, I will never forsake you. You hold my heart in your hands. With these words, I make you a sacred vow that as much as it is within my power, I will never hurt you or turn my back on you. And as soon as I can, I will make a home with you. Together we will build a family." He lifted my hands and kissed my knuckles, one hand at a time. "With my body I will honor and love you, from this day forward. For all time."

I wasn't trying to hold back my tears anymore. I sniffled and used our joined hands to clear my eyes before I took my turn.

"I, Caroline Jane Rogers, take you, Tom, to be my own forever. I promise that I will take care of you, I will listen to you, I will love you and be true to you as long as I live. With my body and my spirit and my mind, I will cherish you for all time. There will never be a minute when my heart doesn't beat for you and you alone. No matter how far apart we are, I am and always will be yours. Nothing in the world, neither life nor death nor distance nor war will change how much I love you." I inhaled deep, shuddering. "My body is yours. It always has been, even before I knew you. I will honor you and love you from this day forward, for all time."

To my astonishment, Tom was crying, too. He let go of my fingers for a minute and pulled at the thin gold band he'd always worn on his right hand. When it came loose, he dropped the ring onto the palm of his opposite hand.

"This is—was— my father's wedding band. He wore it every day, as long as I can remember, until he and my mom were killed in that accident. He told me once that lots of men didn't see the need to wear wedding bands, because they didn't want to appear to be tied down. But he also said he knew the greatest honor and privilege in his life was being attached to my mother. He said he didn't look at it as being tied down; he saw it as a way to prove that the two of them belonged to each other." Lifting the ring reverently, he took my hand and slid it onto my left ring finger. "Caroline, with this ring, I thee wed. I belong to you, and you to me, now and forever."

The gold was warm on my skin, even though it was very loose. I closed my fingers into a fist to keep the ring from falling off and held it up. "Tom. This is beautiful. Are you sure—I don't want to take it away from you."

"I want you to have it." He smoothed my hair back. "There's not much I can give you just now. A week of my time. Letters. And my promises. I want you to take one tangible piece of me home with you." He raised my hands to his lips again, this time kissing the band of gold on my finger. "I have my mother's ring, too, but not with me. Aunt Cissy has it in the safe at home. But one day, when I'm back for good, that one will be yours as well." He grinned at me, although his eyes were still suspiciously red. "Maybe we can trade then. But for now, you hold onto this one. Save it for me. If you want to put it on a chain or have it fit, go ahead. Just promise me you'll always wear it."

"This is the most important gift anyone has ever given me." I clasped my hands and tucked them beneath my chin. "I wish I had something to give you."

"You gave me your picture. And you gave me the most wonderful week of R & R any guy could want. Those memories are better than anything you could buy."

Sighing, I turned in his arms to look up to the falls again. Tom pulled me back against his chest, and for several minutes, we stood together without speaking.

"Someday, when we've been married twenty years, we'll come back to this spot. We'll stand here and remember what it felt like when everything was uncertain and we didn't know if we'd ever see each other again. We'll laugh, because we'll know we never have to be apart again."

"And we'll cry, too, because we'll remember what it was like to have to say good-bye." I laid my head back against his shoulder.

"Our kids will be here with us, and they'll tease and say, 'Wow, our parents sure are saps.'" Tom wrapped his arms more securely around my waist.

"But all the time, secretly they'll love it, because it'll remind them of all the old stories we've told them through the years, about how much in love we were. And still are."

"Will we tell them that we came to Hawaii together before we were married?" Tom's voice was curious. "Won't they be scandalized?"

"We'll tell them, because we'll always tell our kids the truth, about everything. And they won't be traumatized at all. They'll respect us."

"I think I like our future kids."

I giggled. "What's not to like? They're going to be the best of you and me. And we're both pretty terrific."

"True."

"Tom?" I laced my fingers together over his hands. "Is this really going to happen? Do we have a chance for a future?"

"Of course we do." The confidence in his voice was steadying. "This is just a little blip on the screen of our lives. Someday the tough times will be in our past, and our only problem will be figuring out what to name the next baby. I'm partial to Susannah, by the way."

"I like that one, too."

"Hey, Caroline?"

I twisted my neck to look up at him. "Hmmm?"

"Let's go back to the hotel now. We have about twelve hours to make some more memories. I don't want to waste a single second."

~~~***~~~

Throughout the seven days we'd shared in Hawaii, we had never set the small white alarm clock next to our bed. But the next morning, it went off at five, before the sun was even up.

It was a superfluous sound, though, since both Tom and I had been awake long before the clock emitted its insistent tone.

Tom reached across me to switch off the alarm, returning us to the painful silence we'd been keeping for the past hour, since the last time we'd made love. Just as on that night we'd met back in New Jersey, I'd burst into tears as I'd come, heaving sobs shaking both of us as Tom held me tight.

"I don't want to go back." His voice was low and hoarse. "God, Caroline. I don't want to go back there. I don't want to leave you, and I sure as hell don't want to go back to that place."

He hadn't spoken much at all about what it was like in Vietnam. When I'd asked, he'd said he didn't want to think about it while we were together. I'd understood and hadn't pushed. Now I wondered if I should have made him talk more.

"It's bad, isn't it?" I held him a little closer, as though I could protect him from the war raging across the ocean.

"It's . . . it can be bad. But not all the time. In Saigon, life is almost normal, and I think that's worse. We get lulled into feeling like everything is all right, and then something happens and we know it isn't." He traced absent-minded circles on my arm. "And out in the countryside, it's different. This war isn't like any other one the United States has fought before. All the older guys, the officers, say the same thing. There's no front. There's nothing we're defending, really. We're just . . . there. Occupying, sort of. Taking up space. We don't know who to trust, because the same person who gives you directions one day can be setting a bomb in the tent the next."

Fear and trepidation roiled in my stomach. "Maybe it won't last much longer. Didn't they stop bombing North Vietnam last month? I thought they were trying to negotiate peace."

Tom snorted. "Yeah, we stopped bombing them, but they didn't stop sending troops down into the south. One of the gunnery sergeants told me that he'd heard most of the countryside was under VC control now. They just keep coming, you know? And we can't stop them. Not for anything. So we're just holding on where we can, pretending there's some chance of us making a difference."

There was desperation and despair in his words. I struggled to figure out how to offer him comfort. "If all that's true, surely they won't keep you there, will they? They'll pull out soon. Why would we stay and put our boys in danger, if there's no chance of making a difference?"

"We don't pull out. We stay to the bitter end, because we've never lost a war, and we're not going to start here. We're keeping the world safe from communism, you know. If Vietnam falls, then China has a stronger foothold, and God only knows what happens next."

I ran my tongue over my lips. "But it doesn't make any sense."

"War seldom does, babe. I mean, I know why we had to fight in Europe and Asia during World War Two. But we had fronts there. We had support. You know the French were in Vietnam before we were, and they couldn't win anything. But we're so much better."

Rolling to my side, I pushed up to see his face more clearly. "Do you have to stay the whole year? Can't you just . . . quit?"

A smile without much humor curved his lips. "That's not how it works, babe. I'm there until they send me home or . . . well. One way or the other."

"Don't you dare say that." I pounded on his chest with my fist. "You're coming home to me, do you hear, Tom Lawson? I swear, I'll go over there myself and take care of things. You are going to get through your time in Vietnam, and then you're coming back to me. You promised me a future, remember? You're not breaking that promise. If you do, I will be so damn mad at you."

Tom laid his palm on my cheek. "Okay, baby. Calm down. I'm not about to risk the wrath of Caroline Rogers. I'll be fine. I'm going to make it home to you."

I turned my lips to press into his hand. "You'd better."

"I'm sorry." He pulled me back into his arms and kissed the top of my head. "I shouldn't have said anything to you. I didn't mean to make it sound so bad."

"No, I want you to tell me the truth. I want you to be able to talk to me. But never think about— about not making it home, okay? I can't take that."

"I promise." He brushed his lips down my cheek and along my jaw. "I have too much to lose to even think about doing anything else."

"That's better." I sat up, hugging my legs. "Just remember all of this."

"I will." Tom sat up, too, stretching. "Guess we better get moving. I have to finish packing, and then we have to check out of the hotel. I need to be at the USO center on time if I'm going to make the plane back."

We moved through the next few hours in quiet preoccupation. I folded clothes into my suitcase, dread building with each time I emptied a drawer. For seven glorious days, my things had been mingled with Tom's in a wonderful but all-too-short mirage of the forever we both wanted. And now it was over.

He carried my bag and his to the rental car and then came back to the room. "Are you ready?"

"I guess." We stood in the doorway. "Do we really have to leave? We could live here, right? Just hide away in this room?"

"It would be more comfortable than living in the trees, but I'm pretty sure they'd find us even faster." He slid his arms around me. "I know we'll say good-bye at the center, but let me kiss you here. Really kiss you."

Our lips met, open and seeking, and I wished with every fiber of my being that it was a week ago. That our time together was only beginning, not coming to an end. I clung to his shoulders, pulling him as close to me as I could as our tongues tangled.

"God, I love you, Caroline. Never doubt it. I love you with every beat of my heart." He rained kisses over my cheek and when he came back to my mouth, I tasted the salt of my own tears there.

"I love you, too. Promise me again, Tom. Promise you're coming back."

"I do." He rested his forehead on mine. "Those vows we said yesterday . . . they mean everything to me. Remember that. You are my wife in every important sense of the word. In every way that matters, you are mine."

"You are my husband more than James ever was. I meant everything I said to you. You know more about who I am than anyone else in the world."

We remained holding each other for a few more minutes, before Tom reluctantly pulled away. "If I don't get to the USO on time, I won't make my flight back, and then I'll get in trouble and have to be there even longer. The sooner I get back to Vietnam, the sooner I can come home to you."

We closed the door to the hotel room without looking back again.

~~***~~

It was the same group of people, more or less, as it had been a week before in the USO waiting room. The only difference was that this time, all of us women were hanging onto our serviceman with every bit of our desperate strength. We weren't waiting for them to arrive this time; we were dreading their departure.

In the corner, a young woman who was noticeably pregnant sat sobbing into her husband's shoulder. He stroked her back and whispered into her ear, but nothing he was saying made her cry any less. Nearby, a slightly older lady sat with a toddler on her lap, while her husband held their son. I heard him reminding the boy to take of his mother and sister, that he was the man of the family until his dad got home. I felt extraordinarily sad for that little boy, bearing that kind of responsibility.

Tom and I barely spoke beyond small meaningless words. He asked if I had enough money for the taxi to the airport—which I did. I promised to write as soon as I got home, to mail the letter from the airport, even, so that he'd know I'd made it safely as soon as possible.

We'd called his aunt Cissy the day before, and as he'd suggested, I'd even gotten on the line to say hello. She was warm and friendly, inviting me to come visit her in California and asking me to telephone her once I'd gotten settled back at home, just so we could get to know each other better.

"If you need anything at all, call Cissy." He played with a strand of my hair. "I know that sounds crazy, but if I can't be around to help you, she can." He lowered his voice. "If something were to happen—if you did turn out to be pregnant after this week, call Aunt Cissy and she'll help you work out going to California. She'd take care of you until I can."

I nodded. "I will, but I don't think it's doing to be an issue. It was only that one time without—well, you know. And I've been on the Pill for years."

"Still, things happen. Don't be scared if it turns out you're having a baby. I'd never leave you alone with that responsibility."

"I know."

Outside, a bus rolled up to the curb. A groan of dread rolled over the room, and the pregnant girl wailed.

"I can't drag this out." Tom stood up, hefting his bag over his shoulder. "I can't stand here and hold onto you, knowing I have to let go. I'm going to get on the bus now." He held out his one free arm. "Kiss me one more time, and then go out and get your taxi. Don't look back. And the next time we see each other, there won't be any more good-byes for us. We'll be on our way to forever."

I managed to shake my head and lift my lips to his. Tom pressed his mouth against me, all the time murmuring the same words. "I love you, baby. I love you."

He released me, and although I wanted to hold on, I wanted to latch onto his arm and never let go, I forced myself to step back. I pasted on what I was fairly certain was a horrible parody of a smile and gave him a fast wave.

"Good-bye, Tom. Thank you for the best week of my life. I love you. Please, please be safe."

He opened his mouth as though to answer me, but in the end, he only nodded and turned away, walking with long strides toward the door, toward the bus that would carry him to the airplane that would take him far away from me.

I wanted to chase after him and press my face to the glass, sobbing as most of the other women in the room were doing. But I'd made a promise, and I was going to keep it. So instead, I walked to the opposite side of the room, to the door that led to the street.

But I didn't go out right away. I needed to hear the bus leave. I had to be near him as long as I could, even if he couldn't see me and wouldn't know that I was there. I knew.

I didn't turn around even as the sound of weeping swelled. It felt like an eternity before the engine of the bus roared to life, the brakes squeaking and groaning, and then it pulled away. In its wake, the silence was deafening.

I let myself look back over the waiting room one more time. The lady with the two kids had moved over to the corner and was comforting the pregnant woman. Two others were staring out the windows at the taillights of the departing bus.

Before I gave into temptation and sank into a seat to cry, I opened the door and stepped back outside into the bright sunshine. I didn't belong with that crowd. Not yet. They were wives, sisters and parents, and as much as Tom and I might have considered that our vows at Waimea meant something, they hadn't changed me into an Army wife. I didn't have the same rights as those women. I wasn't one of them.

My thumb brushed over the gold band Tom had slipped onto my finger the day before, and I felt a surge of hope. I wasn't his wife, it was true, but we'd made promises. We had a thousand tomorrows to share. I just had to hold on long enough to reach them.

In my mind, I heard his voice, whispering in my ear as we'd stood among the orchids and the birds of paradise.

Save it for me.

Clutching my hand closed, I held tight to the ring and to the promise as I began the long journey toward our future.

Caroline and Tom's story continues in
three more books:
Ain't Too Proud To Beg
California Dreamin'
All You Need Is Love
Coming in 2017

Don't miss their beginning:
More Than Words
Baby, I'm Yours

Author's Note

Writing about the Vietnam War is difficult when the genre is romance or erotic romance. That era wasn't an easy one, and it often conjures uncomfortable or painful memories for us as a people.

When I wrote Tom and Caroline's first story, *More Than Words*, it was only meant to be one book about a couple who met, made a connection and then separated forever. But the idea of these two never meeting again about broke my heart, which is why there was a second book . . . and now a third. And yes, there will be three more.

But while the background of the Vietnam War was fine as a vague idea, a sort of plot device, in the first book, once we moved on, it had to get real. Tom is part of an army fighting in a foreign country without any clear objective. He's dealing with the frustration, fear and pain that all of the soldiers there felt. And Caroline is part of a home-front that didn't understand what was going on or how to respond to it.

This book was a meant to be a reprieve for both of them. I grew up hearing about R & R, what it was like, and I wanted to capture a bit of that for them. For the most part, this couple could pretend that the world around them wasn't imploding. They stole this time, and they lived it to the max. I think that, too, was fairly typical for this era and place.

I don't take a stand on the political aspects of the war in Southeast Asia. I do, though, feel passionately about our veterans, and I hope we all know now that the men and women fighting in Vietnam suffered and continue to suffer for the decisions of those above them.

58,209 men and women gave their lives in Vietnam. 1,643 remain missing or unaccounted for in Vietnam. As a nation, we should never forget them. Please support your local veterans in whatever way you can. If you have the opportunity, visit the Traveling Vietnam Memorial War and/or the Vietnam Memorial Wall in Washington, D.C.

I had the chance to visit the Traveling Vietnam Memorial War right after I finished this book. I hope you will do the same; touch the names and say a prayer for those who will never come home.

More About Emma . . .

Emma Fallon is a southern girl with a penchant for long nights under the stars with hot men. She writes and reads erotic romance and has a special weakness for historical erotica. She can be enticed to do just about anything. . .as long as there's chocolate involved.

Follow her on Facebook! And on Twitter. . . Keep up with her on her website. . . . . .and finally, subscribe to her special events newsletter for the chance to win prizes and get sneak previews of books!

Save It For Me Play List

Save It For Me Frankie Valli and The Four Seasons
Unchained Melody   The Righteous Brothers
Go Now   The Moody Blues
Cherish   The Association
Lightening Strikes   Lou Christie
A Groovy Kind of Love   Mindbenders
Sweet Pea   Tommy Roe
My World Is Empty Without You The Supremes
This Diamond Ring Gary Lewis and the Playboys
Bye Bye Baby Frankie Valli and the Four Seasons

Printed in the USA
CPSIA information can be obtained
at www.ICGtesting.com
JSHW031715140824
68134JS00038B/3703

9 781682 307199